AF580341

ART OF WORDS

BY

ODE CLEMENT IGONI

CALM STORM Publishing
Cover design by: Kosuni Harrison Igoni

TABLE OF CONTENT

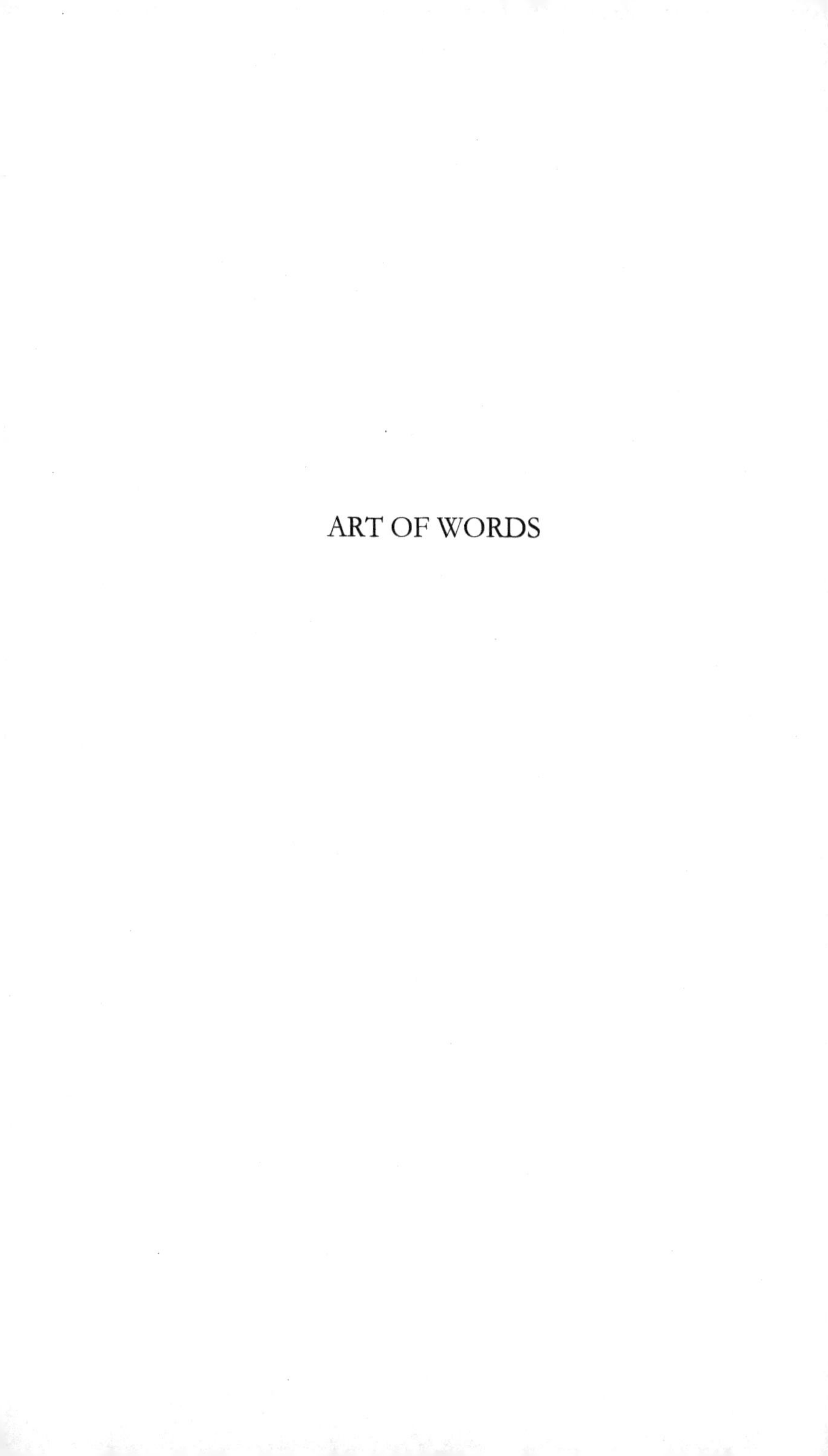

ART OF WORDS

WANDERING

Walking following the sun as my compass
Going from daylight turning unto daylight
No time for night as I keep search for right
Wandering around on earth fallen from high
What to feed the soul as energy drains daily
Sounds of bird chirps quench deep hunger
I wander looking for vessel to be stronger
Beauty and nature to love I wish for daily

Passing through narrow aiming for top
Wandering I try to find myself, I'm lost
From years of weeping and dust to dust
Climbing up the mountain to see how far
Longest distance to the core of a heart
Divergent road, complex and crisscross

Wandering, untrue direction to set point
Morning flowers deceiving as they flaunt
I keep wondering till truth strikes like a gun
Words to justify actions being carried out
Retracing steps to path leading to destiny
Keeping prints for new coming generation

Arriving a point the adventures then cease
Greatest of peace as the leaves turn green
To everlasting the heart is happy and smile
Reaching fixed place after long wandering

A NEW WORLD

In this old world powers forming one
Up in the sky the angels work to bond
We all in line listening to a single voice
The enemy will keep planning to strike
Downfall in economy as food price hike
Virus attack to lock down wide minds
Creeping deep, is there a mind vaccine
Fear of freedom, old dictators as rulers
Forming a transition to liberated thinking
Positive ways of life the best of medicine

Adversity arising, boost to climb the wall
Limits to imagination causing blindness
Struggles for food the stomach will feed
So much portion to toil in this open field
Skill of the hand and creativity from God
Want first and front waiting to be called
Entering a place the world comes from
Opportune to see futures yet to come

I see a brand new world, time don't tick
No struggles or thin, harvests are thick
Birds flying singing sweet songs I know
King sitting up high, none can overthrow
Faces on the street moving with a smile
No hurries or haste cause time don't fly

ROAD TO ETERNITY

Life is a road somedays accident occur
We can never tell at what point it bends
Sweet bitter memories along to recall
Mysteries, tarred floor some can't feed
A journey taking some to unwanted end
Acts and events I look out the window
As I keep travelling maintaining my lane
We turn to bones on the road to eternity

Speeding in life, God controls the wheel
Steering me to a desired point on course
Driving me through time no pause to refuel
Gaining it all until the end which is vanity
The spirit is oblivious as it transcend further
Leaving behind bones as eternity continues

Road to eternity, emotions receives shock
Pains to absorb and happiness for a smile
Destination unknown retracing to find God
Driving through life as the season changes
With eyes on focus still facing challenges
The sky being blue, my greatest motivation

On the road to eternity we face perdition
Words and accusations of unknown deeds
Wanting to cause chaos along the journey
I swiftly drift and keep my mind in sanity
Knowing only bones will make eternity

WHISPER OF THE NIGHT

Whisking of the wind flying words around
At very first not seen until motion abound
Listening hearing grave silence in the dark
Whispering images for one eye to see alone
Bringing forth a world that is preserved long
On pages as the memory ceases some day
Or back to one same spot of silence spoken
Words to engrave pictures of what is to come

Whisper of the night reminding me of life
That on a very good day the ball will turn
Still having breathe finally will disintegrate
Memory stored in art for generation to see
How the night whispers connecting souls
One big realm from whence it all comes
Giving words to all I'm keen like an eagle
Arts and pieces to last for a million years

Whisper of the night painting good times
At the mountain top I sit to feel its peak
Deep in the night all dark great light spark
Moving clouds thundering as sky turn red
Scroll being opened as a message is read
Voiceless speaker whispering words to me
The air translate as the night remains quiet
Then I hear "We go to come once again"

CIRCLES

Thick fog humans all turning in circle
Going through stages arriving at same
Fed from bottle as we grow back to baby
Life circles embedded in time and season
In a box gravity as static yet going in circles
As tidal as the wave returning to same point

Producing, more births to come for balance
So is death to come for a complete circle
Events not seen as thousand more to show
The rivers flow making the world go round
Time of shedding and time for gaining weight
Broader horizons to widen my thought circle

When I reproduce, beginning of a new life
Time to be seeing through eyes of offspring
Retracing my steps making better correction
Knowing the wind will blow someday I'm gone
Like leaves falling to preserve a whole system
Living from century to century going in circles

PRINTS

Stamping my foot making prints to last
A voice known when placed on canvas
Drawing paths keeping hints into future
The dice is cast, gunshot, race begins
Going to Wonderful everyone searching
Working to own assets and cash prints

Pictures of years past prints in memory
Times of the good, sad, happy or allegory
Exchanging bloods making new prints
Of my DNA resulting some carbon copy
Coming into a place running eternal race
Living in apartments with rents long paid

Keeping prints recorded in time and space
Clearing paths for many to be next in line
Creating a world to come, things all fine
As the wheel spins through years coming
Beauty of hearts shinning bright in the sky
Showing prints of deeds that's tread earth

NIGHT-TIME

Stars out shinning as the night harmonize
Crickets and frogs singing as I fantasize
Of turning so bright like rainbow in the sky
Very expensive like diamonds, always high
How the moon flies so far yet illuminates
The night turns to gray in a blend of all

Communing with Him who brings it all
Deep in the night behold passing words
Solving big riddles of puzzles that cross
And of understanding to paddle across
From dusk till dawn to move the pawn
There come more ingredients to paint

Dark night all lights turned off still I shine
Imaginations to come in forms and style
In stanzas leading to where there's light
To where the sun rises even in the night
Sipping some tea, staying ever natural
Singing chorus, the night makes sounds

MINDS' EYE

Taking a view of earth coming from sky
Layers of air with different chem-form
Birds, they feed and fly as night is nigh
Streamlined eye to never miss a flight
Towards target time ticks fast onward
Screened writing to see what's forward

Landing in the cold shaking away dust
Ink flows bold creating from mind's eye
New arts and thinking making things hot
Clear detail when one view from the mind
Connecting the eye, God's gift given to all
Special link to emotions, feelings for more

Navigating through forests crossing lakes
A bright mind always going to better days
Two eyes put to use in feeding the mind
Connecting cognitive, seeing in numbers
Keeping on pages no extent of mind's eye
Travelling on earth seeing clearer in time

FREEDOM

Chained to a way of life with adopted thinking
A thrown history from past cleaning all trace
Burnt in fire, words and images go in flame
Chained mind knowing only what is shown
Bloody annexation changing trade activities
Africa Lion going roars, only ancestors tame

A journey across centuries seeing it all
Fighting to wipe remnants of bitter history
Freedom of speech bringing back stories
Setting sail no limit everyone's voice soar
Growing, once a slave now owning trees
Once a planter going on to own hectares

Change is come no colors everyone equal
Getting closer to the sun complexion black
Melting negative thoughts, bad influences
Journey of breaking free from past slavery
Treading on pure ground not making sound
Freedom as souls from old start jubilating

BONES

Silence, no sounds as the spirits they walk
Bones scattered, dead economy can't talk
Years of grass expecting grace to come
Twenty one added to two thousand gone
Archeologist still discovering new bones
Carbon-dating into past of humans form

Looking for divine ways to rise new throne
Fueling the economy and revive lost souls
Adding flesh to cover dryness from trickle
Even as national legislators go on to dribble
Killing this nation forgetting values of lives
Can't take away words from poets giving life

Time for humans to rise forming large army
One voice singing choruses, no more sorrow
Love and unity, blood that keeps us growing
Thinking hard like iron to create better future
Digging, planting seeds to bloom happiness
Years to come bones stand clapping hand

IN THE RAIN

Dancing in the rain washing tears of pain
Looking in your eyes to wipe sorrow away
Getting wet along time sacrifice to be paid
Journey from past I swipe to a new frame
Holding hands we stroll down to forever
Of smiles and happiness, the sun shines

Dancing in the rain as we come back home
Savoring moments of life that never fades
We are free playing like kids our kids grown
Hearts close knitted two surviving as one
Creating warmth, cold night down the hill
Beating in love my heart wants your feel

Dancing in the rain your hips and curve I see
Spinning sending me back and forth in time
Relinquishing the past we go to better days
Love bonding strong my best till end of age
Your smile keeping me till dawn in the rain
Sensual healing just for you and no one else

WEAKNESS

In my weakness I look deep inside of me
Place to find strength making clear blurs
Effervescence of thoughts to understand
Body may be broken but the mind is alert
To every milliseconds of things that pass
Goosebumps I feel in search to find at last

In weakness my thoughts gives strength
Sitting I ponder where to dig and find oil
Imaginary obstructing I punch and defeat
Fighting hallucinations I stand on my feet
Divine unction power to succeed appears
Spurring out of strength-less to come alive

Keeping me going rising to greater height
Projected flight like rockets flying to sky
Going into sun to find searching all place
For where abundance is stored and refills
Knowledge growing so beautiful on trees
Peace and beauty of life giving strength

HILL OF UNKNOWN

Long long time ago across Hill of Unknown
There standing a tree its seed do not grow
Leaves that sheds every passing of moon
Tears locked in branches wanting offshoot
Ground so dry thousands of years no rain
A house is found and where its keeper lay

Voices echo as shrubs anew they sprout
Eyes lurking like the wolves around it roam
Of cries and fangs everyone gnashing atop
Destinations unknown souls return to sow
Attached in blood many come and time go
Identities hanging on the road to perdition

On the Hill of Unknown walking endlessly
Safeguarding thinking I take on to eternity
World riches when breathe goes is vanity
Some world leaders go on acting ruthless
Forgetting we go out of existence someday
Meeting at journey across Hill of Unknown

ONE

One to my one making life complete in two
Face and smile special, made for one alone
Into my heart it goes my love begins to burn
Wanting a blend of mix making perfect form
Two strokes of traits bringing new next turn
On the alter professing as we join in accord

Trials and set pits, we jump crossing over
One minute hands on knob rocketing away
Emotions growing stronger than hard rock
Touch from you melts annoyance and grief
In your eyes I see truest of heart from belief
You alone I hold on to time of passing over

Deep in sleep I am awake to consciousness
Of your heart beating following palpitations
Tingling's stirring feelings to arouse into you
Copulating bring forth ones male or female
Reflection of lives breathing through one
Life makes meaning with the perfect one

BURNING FIRE

Walking through fire to refine my thoughts
Old ways of thinking melted to form iron ore
Strong views and visions showing money core
Burning away laziness, enviness causing lost
Screenshot rays showing directions to come
As words are being razed going into thin air

A thousand degree the fire never quenches
Year to year it keeps flaming passing to next
Like relay relating past to a new set of mind
Shinning like diamond gone through inferno
Raising self-value to a net worth high and hot
Flies don't perch on sword hot from smelting

Deep in fire many go through making wealth
Coming out stealth cooling pains from burns
Enjoying harvests reaping from big heat sown
Remaking profits as the fire goes on burning
Fueling activities keeping operations running
A fire going to millenniums and never ending

SPELL

Locked away deep in the ocean of your heart
Drowning for years still I do not die from love
A sweet bitter taste to compensate past hurt
Potion dripping into my lips locking in a spell
Erasing every move causing me wanting out
In your blood I sleep, dream, wake and feast

A spell you cast keeping me forever with you
In your smile your eyes sending out radiation
Thunder to strike any day I try breaking free
A mix of love prepared centuries long ago
Ancient spell bounding us together for life
Keeping the magic stronger across strife

Walking down time to come in agreement
In you I bury my thoughts, in a ground fertile
Unending passion, twists and turns around
Sailing across Mediterranean to distant see
Beauty of love allowed to set sail across sea
Best of images to come locked in your spell

BEYOND HERE

What food for the soul when body is no more
Inheritance to get some die rich some go poor
To a place silence as currency to buy all want
Are there trees and animals for human to hunt
Seeds and sand the eye sees all things as soil
No breath to plant a living dead that can't toil

Beyond here deep down the mind grows again
In lineage to the living as we all see ourselves
Sky holding communication as voices all raise
Singing songs in adoration to a place of soar
Into space scientist go forever keeping search
No signal, a medium high voices are not heard

Beyond here and there someday we all go visit
Residing as single with new faces from bones
Watering earth with traits passed in new form
No return to flesh the spirit has a new home
A place of no return, one way visit to forever
Beyond here a brand new existence to come

RUNNING

Out in morning dew I chase after you
Wings of emotions attached on me I fly
Running chasing your deepest feeling
Innermost of your heart painting love

Beautiful inside of you I go on to feel
Thudding of heart like down with ill
Heal all over like fragrance released
My heart marathons a thousand mile

Running beside you I dream of each day
As life unfolds in babies and packages
Through farm life planting seeds to grow
One day we all fade for new life to blow

I'll keep running with you till end of ways
When air is gone all that's left are tracks

SOAR

Closer to end facing obstacles I bend
The spirit is free going jumping hurdles
On run way picking high speed for lift
Enemy coming my lane I turn and drift
Bid to become the best along my path
Time from creep, walk, going up high

Let the wind point directions to soar
As my thinking's go higher no lower
Spread wings and then begins to fly
Far Into sky like eagle on speed flight
High in the clouds moving with birds
Words gone up landing on mountains

Fly high looking at earth from distance
Rights and wrongs all kept in instance
Falling thoughts, flapping to clear sight
Of all that's good and what is to come
Rising generations shine bright like star
We all end this life soaring far up in sky

CALM

In scorching heat exposed to hot sun
Toiling all day putting roof over head
Placing food on the table, basic need
Chasing hunger with a balanced meal
To calm stomach making loud sound
Man and working, together long bound

Saving for rainy times not having much
In the dark searching for way with torch
Relaxed, calm, not kicking foot to injury
Things not going right, I switch off fury

Reduce stress of life each passing day
Rewarding time input as currency pay
Taking vacation to sea cruising top way
Break from all to calm down brain relay
Sipping a tot as sharks all come to play
Calm waves of life, things in proper stay

INFINITY

Unique words spread around to all poets
Its source and origin comes from infinity
Divinity through distinct voice and words
Bringing to tangible the spirit of arts in all

Medium showing pictures of fine arts
We only find when gotten from real one
Across different nation, colors and race
Documenting history of past and future

One source from which all words spring
Unseen voice in images of arts to keep
Priceless going far to new millenniums
Hung on walls in galleries and in minds

I am a poet painting arts with my words
Inspirations lifelong coming from infinity

SERENDIPITY

WHAT'S NOT LOST

Air we breathe keeps the lungs longer
The feelings of wanting to fill hunger
The mouths that are dry and thirsty
Those that stay happy grow stronger

Voices are saying "Don't push further"
Spirits working hard injecting negativity
Deep in the minds of the young at heart
Painting times of stagnation and failure

What's not lost is the button to start
I'll turn mine on and drive till the end
Through time of doubt and challenges
Thoughts of climbing higher is not lost

The drive for success laid in the heart
Is the greatest of things that can't be lost

ONE TOUCH

One touch from you sends a burning fire
A feeling that has been my one desire
Your strokes so sensual I cannot resist
It goes from top to the bottom of the sea

That moment in time I am all yours
Picture so divine I won't skip a frame
A body of art created by him above
Feelings all loosed, only you can tame

Emotions beginning to run into the wild
It's been searching from far and wide
Finding a way to calm these tide
And also to bring forth a child

I can't forget memories of your touch
A thousand of them come in one touch

WHEN ALL IS SAID AND DONE

When all is said and done we become mute
When life has squeezed from us all the fruit
There is nothing left to be done hence we go
To a place no one knows but everyone goes

All the stress and worries about tomorrow
While asleep the hair on our head still grow
No matter the situation faced time still goes
Cause its goal is for when all is said and done

I'll fix my eyes on the climax, final moment
Then I have a picture of all what I've done
All what I've said along this journey I'm on
Flashing in my memory as I go up the stair

After all is said and done we are still flesh
An organic matter that goes on to decay

LINE

With open arms I offer you a hug
Together we'll win this tug of war
We can pull the world to our side
Sit on it enjoying joyous moments

You hold my vein, the thinnest line
Keep holding it I'm doing just fine
My heart is beating, feel the pulse
Take the keys and pin to the purse

A thin line between life and death
Let's stay alive, happy and together
Living a peaceful life free of regret
Working diligently till it gets best

I've dreamed of this time for so long
When we run the race till finish line

PURE HEART

If only we maintain pure heart like a baby
We'll make our world stable as we grow
A heart free from hate for each other
There won't be killings or annexation

Let love come and cleanse the land
Washing away the roots of confusion
So we can all sing songs as one band
Everyone keeping his right proportion

If we maintain pure heart as we grow
The land will blossom green as rivers flow
We'll be happy as we hear the cock crow
Ushering to us a new day filled with honey

Let our thoughts pause and have a rebirth
Putting away bad, welcoming a pure heart

SUMMER TIME

It is summer time let's go meet the sun
Come along with your daughter and son
Let's go to the beach and catch some fun
I've got energy from the sun to lift a ton

It's summer time, cold no longer found
Bright and radiating day is what I want
There's joy all around village and town
As kids ride their bicycles round town

Summer time ushers in happiness
Families bonding more during picnics
Smiles found on the faces of children
As they take a long break from school

It is summer time I'm feeling new
Sunbathing, my energy is renewed

LISTENING

Listening to my thoughts as I wander
It's guiding me beyond unto yonder
I keep deaf ears to rumors and slander
We are all in sin city trying to survive

When things get too difficult I ponder
On the street some lives are begging
Empty stomach but still they're moving
With the hopes to make life in the city

Listening to my thoughts I avoid blunder
It tells me to be calm during the storm
It's all a process that makes up the form
I'm listening closely to navigate the sea

The words may come then disappear
I'll be keen and hear directions to follow

SHIELD ME

Shield me with your love in this battle of life
Absorb the shocks during my time of little
Stay strong to keep our relationship floating
During times our tears increases the ocean

Shield me from the pains to hurt my soul
At every gate I'm willing to pay the toll
Protect me from my head to my sole
As we entangle with friends and foe

I have made a vow to shield you forever
From the beginning down up till ever
You're my medicine that cures this fever
I feel your love even inside my liver

As we go through these walls together
The love we share will shield us forever

STROKES

With words I paint this journey I'm on
As I strike barriers and gently glide
Coming from the past of nothing
Till my image fills up the canvas

The enemy constantly sends strokes
I do my best to avoid being in their flow
Steadfastly walking into the future
Where my visions become realities

With my hands I'll diligently paint strokes
From desert years until the grass is green
To a time beauty covers the whole world
Billions of faces all covered with a smile

We all got feet's treading earth's surface
Let's put up a beautiful image of footprints

WAR

Before a man can stand on his feet
He first crawls then learn to walk
Facing war as he aims for the top
Hands of gravity pulling him back

Battles to fight, hurdles to jump
Heights to climb, oceans to cross
Will there ever be glorious days
When economy takes hope away

From all corners the war comes
Emotional, financial and lots more
All clamoring to be resolved
Time doesn't wait, it ticks on

With knowledge fight the battles
Till a time there is no more war

SINKING

I am sinking please come save me
My tears is washing away images
Of smiles and laughter's we had
Looking at you and being glad

I see your spirit reaching forth to me
Wanting to pull me out of the pool
To rescue the good years we shared
Bringing back the time we were cool

I was sinking and needed your love
You stood by watching me go deeper
Through a point of erasing memories
Down this black hole having no end

If only you stretched forth your arm
You would have rescued this heart

IN YOUR HEART

Keep me locked forever in your heart
That's where I want to spend my time
In the cell of your Love I appreciate
The warmest of place to feel care

I'm happy spending years in your blood
Through the thin and thick as it unfolds
My hands you let free to move around
More and more in your spell I'm bound

Lock me in your heart and throw the key
I'm willing to perish in your deep forever
Cause there our hearts will beat as one
Then we bring generations next to come

Locked in your heart our blood flow is one
It's where I want to be till years count out

RUNNING

Running to protect my head from bombs
Falling from the sky to terminate earth
The reason for chaos is still unknown
Yet many nations go to war fully armed

The hand holding earth begins to weary
Its climate has been filled with toxic
Acids dropping from the sky in raindrops
Where do I run to in times of rainfall

I take cover in the mountain, it rains there
I go to the ocean, the fishes are all dead
Bullets raining heavily in the desert
That's why there are no grasses green

I keep running away from the rain
To a place I find peace and sunlight

PEACE

Peace of the night, come calm my soul
Sleepless nights can't hunt me no more
With you by my side I feel so strong
I may be short but this love's so long

Peace of the night bring chills down my bone
I can't let you go through the night all alone
Sweet and high like pills in my blood stream
The world stands still as you give your smile

Peace of night as we cuddle long hours
Killing the hunting and daunting of cold
Images the heart draw, so sweet and bold
Peace of the night brings forth cute flowers

In the dark I clearly see the peace you bring
Sensation soothing, that's why I still sing,

FAR

The good life I dream may seem far away
I'll streamline it, making sure I don't sway
My passion will take me to a time of full
Seeing through the needle eyes of the bull

Looking at a point far and bring it close
Working had all day taking the full dose
Empty pocket days that will need filler
Working hard every day, is my healer

Consistency I know takes me to big dream
With persistence, we'll form the best team
Looking at the mirror and seeing my face
Closing up the place then I fly into space

Up in the sky far away with big dreams
Picture wide and long that takes me far

SMILE

Your smile at dawn brightens up my day
Through it all we are here forever to stay
Your voice lightens up a fire from spark
Your touch detonates feelings from lack

Your smile snaps thin feelings held back
Gushing out wants to stop bleeding heart
Love and motions all flowing from red hot
A burning fire being quenched with a smile

Your smile shines so bright up in the sky
I see it every day, a reason why I'm here
Together we can go from here to there
Where there is happy hearts and health

You've got the magic inside of you
It comes out each day when you smile

UNSEEN HAND

Onward we march into the dark motivated
Going past the beasts that wish to eat man
Shedding blood to correct wrongs of past
Fighting to make the human race elevated

An unseen hand standing fighting with us
Striking the enemy that tries to stop us
Howls of the wolves deep in the night
The moon shines to show us our path

We fall asleep when the sun goes down
In solidarity the hand keeps watch at night
Placing a hedge around our resting point
Keeping us safe all night in a wide palm

In a time of weary we keep pushing on
An unseen hand backing us to win it all

LOOK DEEP

Look deep inside me and see my desire
It's you I'll hold as we go through the fire
Getting burned to last for much longer
As we stay hard keeping away -mongers

Look deep and see my feelings brewing
Reach inside, fetch love till satisfaction
From the well of my heart draw my love
It keeps flowing up until the end of time

Look deep into your heart for reflections
Throwing back images of pure intentions
Planted feelings growing into love forest
From long ago we've passed all set test

Once a shallow mind now with deep roots
Going deep into your heart looking at love

AMBITION

When the journey I'm on faces stormy days
My ambition takes the wheel and it steers
Through barriers and obstacles to jump
It keeps me going as long as blood pumps

In time of nothing I keep up with smiles
Heading to a time the tides will be over
Planting seeds to grow a large vision
That spurs this engine of my ambition

My ambition is to get the best from earth
Diligently following laid out plans in coffers
Of my mind holding values reaching future
When all work done comes back profitable

I'll stick to my goal on this field of life
Working to fulfill ambitions despite strife

FOUNTAIN

In the desert I found a fountain of love
Drinking to refresh in the scorching sun
An empty heart roaming till it finds care
Once fell so deep into the darkest of lair

I'll build myself around your peaceful world
Never to run dry from the sweet of your word
Flowing into millions of years yet to come
Your fountain of love gives me utmost peace

Drinking from your love that never dries
Rejuvenating years my world was so dry
Bringing back my health, emotions and life
As I bask in this fountain of your great love

Through many years of drought searching
Bringing me to this place and I won't leave

OBLIVION

APART

Gave you my all and you tear it apart
Now you want to come into my heart
Going back from the end to the start
The heavy pulse of my love's gone flat

Was in the dark, needed your love as light
Dreaming of time when we shine so bright
Broke my heart, next thing you took a flight
Gone for many years I can't find my sight

Whole world shredding, you tore me apart
My heart is bleeding I can't find my path
Since you left nothing done seems right
I keep search looking to heal this patch

I'm burning in the desert, the sun's so hot
Wishing for your love to come off my heart

SACRIFICE

I lay down my heart chopped in pieces
On this table as I offer my love to you
I'll take the fall for mistakes you made
Spending all my years locked in your jail

I accept to share my future that's with you
I'll sacrifice a great part of my heart for you
Making sure you're covered from life's rain
That fall drops of hardship on some days

I've sacrificed from the past, more to come
This way our love keeps shining like the sun
Growing nations from our loins to come
Caring for each other as we make sacrifices

Faced with same decisions I stand firm
I'll keep sacrificing to keep our hearts

RIVERS

Rivers of Love that flows from creeks
Diverse of tongues all living in peace
Trees in the forest shinning so green
With roots tapping deep into the river

Rivers of love that flows to the city
Gone are years of angst and deceit
Many voices forming one in truce
Ending sounds of guns in the bush

My state of mind with treasure's base
Processed crude thinking to oil my feet
Generating revenues for me in this city
Becoming the garden city of my world

A state I find several of good thoughts
Rivers state, base of oil feeding nations

WIND OF YEARS

Wind of years passing through my lens
Doubling the years multiplying the tense
Struggles may make the weight dense
Spoils from victory, what my soul yearns

Wind of years as I climb up the stairs
Keeping more peaceful healthy affairs
Closing good deals, toasting and cheers
Joyous moments with me and all my peers

Wind of years as I begin to hold a stick
A million miles, time still goes on to tick
Taken many roads, through a forest thick
Deeply rooted in thoughts, now hard like brick

Wind of years blowing to now and beyond
Bringing back feelings I thought was gone

WILD FIRE

A tree rising high up into the sky
Birds all scattered, the children fly
Energy sent across through wires
Down to earth burning in wild fires

Kangaroos they leap and try to run
It's already late, flesh begins to burn
Burning from mountains to valleys
Burning homes and animal alleys

Oh how species are razed to ashes
A cold painful sight of bones to see
Of trees all burned, turned to coal
Keeping pictures that can't be erased

Don't show yourself in such manner
Forgive any reason for such wrath

SEARCHING

Digging during the day, sleeping at night
The body needs some rest from searching
What to eat, where to sleep, how to feel
Falling deep but bouncing back to the top

Resetting the mind keeping it safe at sea
Searching for bearing as the compass lead
It's not one day, the very end a must to see
Finding guides and principles I may heed

Searching for the brightest of thoughts
That gives everyone the widest of smiles
On this journey with distinct destinations
Finding solutions each day as way of life

Kept in places far and wide for all to reach
Quest for solutions keeps more questions

I'M GONE

At that point we take different turns
My heart is broken as my love burns
Walking into oblivion our souls depart
Strong bond we share now torn apart

Heavy are my feelings each day I wake
Distorted images, I find peace at the lake
Fun times gone, things begin to feel dead
Chasing a lost love long gone in my head

Through many years of building yet we fall
I go down on my knees but standing tall
I'm gone with the wind to a place far away
All things feel so light as I bend and sway

I'm gone to where I'll drink from true love
I'm gone to where I'll taste true feelings

DEEP DOWN

Deep down in the cave I found gold
Many years of digging, I won't let go
Your precious soul, very dear to me
You have no price, you can't be sold

From deep down your love springs
Into outer space this love ship goes
At the blink of my eye you own me
Your touch sends vibrations to earth

Deep down, your precious heart lies
I'll keep mining till abundance of love
Fragile ground, no one has trampled on
River of love flowing unto years to come

Striking the rock, mining your heart
Deep down is where I want to reach

ONE KISS

One kiss got me spinning around
Dancing from morning till sundown
I keep going in circles turning round
At your feet, final place I bow down

One kiss got me spinning through time
Feelings so deep it's breaking my spine
If you leave this heart stops ticking fine
If you leave this air stops flowing in time

Your kiss brings back moments we've lived
Craving for frames of feelings to be relived
As we come bare, with hands of no stains
Cleaning tears of years filled with pains

One Kiss puts me in the happiest place
I'm willing to stay with you for many years

ONE WAY

This time around I'll take one way home
No need to frown I've got you in my sight
I'll keep to this track that leads to your heart
All of me you own, two lanes becoming one

Going past the narrow wide and dark road
To where your eyes shine showing my way
When faced with toll, I give my heart as pay
Shedding others away as I reduce this load

One way that goes to feeling your heart beat
A road I'll never want my wheels to skid off
Eyes locked on you as I navigate through
To the end where I'll drink from abundance

One way in and out of your sweet heart
Even in the rain I'll follow, lead me home

AROUND THE FIRE

Out in the wild, just me and my lady
A burning desire opens up my heart
Sending out hot radiation that sparks
Falling on grasses they begin to burn

Gazing at the fire as I twist some turn
Sounds of animals all night as melody
In the fire images of passion is seen
In your eyes my final destination I see

Dancing to the rhythm of burning fire
Holding your hand as I bare my heart
Closer to you I move burning emotion
Blood pumping, you put me in motion

Around the fire I stay all night in love
Burning a kiss chasing the cold away

FIXED

Suddenly I wake to hands bound in chains
Bleeding, dripping black blood from pains
Crown made of thongs each step a strike
Rowing through storms and unforeseen hike

Surviving centuries of travelling the world
My mind is fixed to an anchor, my words
Preserved in my blood that is black as crude
Year to years the blood goes on to brood

Freedom is come; I find my way back home
To drill from the wisdom stored deep in earth
Found in vegetation at every region of search
Harnessed at a place directed by knowledge

After long journey of trials and tribulations
My thoughts gets fixed as it returns home

SUNNY DAY

A bright sunny day well-lit by your love
Is how my heart feels when in your arm
Toiling years together filling up our barn
Your smile brings blessings from above

A bright sunny day at the break of dawn
Together we going forward like the pawn
Standing tall defending the world we build
Keeping a level playing ground on this field

Today the sun shines differently, we're one
Simultaneously our hearts beats as one
Feelings all set ablaze from your light
I've got fire; I'll spark and make it bright

Sitting all through the night at the ocean
On this sunny day I release my emotion

REDRAW MY WORLD

On this sand of time I redraw my world
I've been working, walking through walls
Coming out on the other side at the top
Looking down to the world I had drawn

On this sand of time I bury my words
Far and wide I've gone spilling blood
Forming an art that comes from deep
Down in the well rising through the pen

Keeping pictures of thoughts and smiles
Of a tree with offspring's coming out fine
A world filled with so much truth no lies
A world where everything lovely is mine

On this sands of time I march till forever
Changing view looking down gone forever

FALLING

Thrust from the sky falling down to earth
Landing on space all filled up with hate
A place I keep struggling to find my sight
The future to come takes a longer while

A falling economy, many souls drowning
Unfulfilled promises, everyone's frowning
Government rescue for a few to survive
Proudly keeping millions in dark nights

Falling deep down into a realm of oblivion
Going back and forth in search of divinity
To come cleanse corrupted ways of thinking
Rising to a stand of good ways and actions

Falling is a time to gain momentum
Bouncing back up to a better start

RUNNING

I'm running, I'm running, away from you
Turned me a fool, thinking we were cool
Gave my all, you pushed me in the pool
Made my heart freeze, kept it in the fridge

This love's gone cold, stories everyone told
Holding your hand walking, still I was bold
Deep thoughts inside you I really don't know
You just pretend being white like the snow

I gave you my heart you gave me your back
I was like a river when I let this love flow
Making it wet when things was so dry
Love you didn't want got locked in a pool

Running away from you to find my way out
I'm losing breath locked up in this abyss

MOVING CLOUD

From dark I travel through lights of time
Through territories bringing break of dawn
Through the moon, through scorching sun
Telling everyone asleep it's time to wake up

Moving through as time flies to no return
Keeping memories of million centuries seen
One big eye that watches all your dreams
Hearing prayers and songs everyone sings

Look up you'll see the different shades of me
I'm here keeping everyone good down there
Drying the tears everyone cries down there
Without me there will be dangers on earth

Moving through infinite keeping us all
Like the waters flowing, beginning to end

INSIDE THE MOON

Together sharing warmth inside the moon
Looking into your eyes morning till noon
World of our own, two hearts counting one
World filled with honey, dancing to drums

The rhythm of our heart now beats as one
No mountains to climb no falling from hills
No gravity, emotions are free to fly wild
Every minute intentions rising so high

I go down on my knee as I usher you in-
to my heart as we fly to honeymoon
Bringing forth kids with flavors to spice
Holding hands from now until afterlife

Inside the moon I find peace holding you
As we live through beautiful years to come

FEELINGS

When it sees you they all jump out happy
Your perfume runs ten thousand crazy
Helter-skelter inside of me wanting out
A touch from you my feelings burst out

Following a road through the narrow path
Reaching inside you going to your heart
Through your stomach leaving offspring's
Breaking the rock bringing water from spring

Living inside you through the curve of life
Different times and turns taking the lead
On this train ride that leads to sweet days
In old days we'll happily share pictures

My feelings for you flow long like the sea
Deeper than top to center of earth's crust

TOUR

When asleep my mind embarks on tour
Going to far places my legs can't reach
Searching for best time that can be kept
Searching for a key that opens the locket

Flying with the eagles across the mountain
Flying with the dolphins exploring the sea
Through the amazon, following the creek
Thereafter going up high reaching the peak

Traveling through time as I control my flight
With closed eyes I go on to find my sight
Soaring in beauty of imagination as I rest
A time my thoughts are free to fly far away

I'm going on tour, no visa no boundaries
Relaxing a stressed mind from much work

ECLECTIC

ABSTRACT

Looking at sky, dark clouds moving so fast
I'm chasing after time don't want to end last
Thoughts and feelings flying out, it all roams
Getting high finding a way to sit top of dome

Wanting good life sun comes shining bright
Abstract image, working to fix broken light
Sticking to large vision walking so cynical
Vibrating of distant thinking coming lyrical

Abstract I see fragments to form one piece
Light passing through lens all I see is peace
Large mural hanging in deepest of my heart
Showing all I want, road to my destiny path

Divine touch to see what I want in whole
Inspiration to keep going covering miles

DYSTOPIA

Many years ago called as leader of morrow
Place the rulers always go foreign to borrow
Keeping huge debts for future unborn to pay
And then they perish leaving behind dark day

Fuel hike, unknown gunmen society in turmoil
Economy in chaos they keep selling crude oil
No remittance as education goes down drain
Much hardship like acids falling down in rain

A nation in dystopia, when will healing show
I go to stream seeing turbulent rivers do flow
Humans praying, we all seeking good people
Calming tides and brings peace to all ripple

Run or to stay, no one loves danger places
Killings of security persons, victims faces

SWING

Swing as we jump going thru downs and up
In the wind free rotates and turns to record
Shaking taking giant strides on choreograph
To rhythms of life beat, the drums all sound

One step take two step forward marching on
Some trips stagger and fall each other to hold
Swing riding high cloud to time immemorial
Soar! Oh how soothing is your companion

Never to crash both hearts anchored to love
Swing through the cold in woods fire spark
On travel and tour in ballet rooms to dance
Keeping to time body twists my brain turns

Around we go what sweet time of the night
Years to more coming I drown in your heart

REHEAT

Quarrels and misunderstanding yet we live
Silence my heart hanging where owls live
At mountain top nests scattered we leave
Deeply injured but do not die nor bereave

Reheat my feelings all come back renewed
Fire burn coming down hill with spirit filled
Cloths of emotions multiple colors shining
No more cold past is done let's go dining

Your smile, spark that brings fire to reheat
Notes of treble so sweet, oh my heart beat
No better gift to man than making whole
Final piece of creation closing puzzle hole

Distance to come a love that never dies
Flames may be low a fire that never dies

FOREFATHERS

One blood we all come from spiritual source
History dating back to beginning of lifetime
Breeding a generation with updated force
Found around all terrestrial and new clime

Reflections of past image in body and soul
One may be dead spirit go on to procreate
New poets with inspiration from forefathers
All alive seeing where the words they go to

Writing keeping footprint of stay on earth
Reincarnate in vessels of pure from birth
Lead footstep to place knowledge is kept
Deep in art where trinity of man anchors

Following set line of craft to future come
One day and I'm gone to my forefathers

RELIGION

Forces of doctrine keeping earth turning
Man is god divine and fire within burning
Searching for directions to meet creator
Some go on and slay becoming dictator

Say a prayer for no one knows tomorrow
Darkness some will dig deep in to burrow
Misled, some shed tears to many sorrow
Ending the long day with a vessel hollow

Man is religion finding the source of light
To living so long years in place of bright
Closing eyes see final realm and height
Ascending spirit and soul gone, no fight

Accepting a path leading to great beyond
Like compass showing what's yet to come

HEART'S EYE

Looking like sparrow in deep of the night
Searching for right vein to channel blood
To keep things moving awaiting the light
Riding on cruise whenever there is flood

Inside narrow finding way to right place
Same group looking as one to make face
Two hearts one eye going the same route
Of hemoglobin, one voice to blow flute

Heart's eye keen to pick part making whole
To bring smiles, new oxygen given breathe
Many years it remains pure and evergreen
Preserved in love, forever it'll never brink

Look through my heart's eye, you to find
Of one blood and pumping to never-end

LET IT RAIN

Cloudy day pocket so dry I cry till dawn
It is going to rain fortunes falling on me
Been through starvation and thirstiness
Reaching persons with mind merciless

Bewildered facing illusions of roadblock
Taking stock of years passing emptiness
Great and mighty of wealthy men I stalk
Waiting for rub off as I break hard-knock

The rain will fall cos I've paid my due
Heavy waters upon me to wake in dew
Soften the ground from heavy drought
End creaking sound my pocket makes

Dancing in the rain from now till ever
Sweet memories here to stay forever

SUN VIEW

Many miles to come before reach of sun
Up in sky green lands keeping for my son
Across sea making tracks for all to see
Advancing I go and all challenges I saw

Climbing mountains reaching my peak
Spectrum of light passing lens of me
Beautiful colors I see sweet like steak
Down the hill is grass I plant some tree

The sun is shining my way time to grow
Springing abundance of seeds I've sown
Reflecting all what to be done and reap
As life winds from one level to bigger

My blood going up in sky more to spill
Look up and see my sun drip with red

WINE

Whining, it's so sweet please make it last
You grinding fast slowly, yea make it sound
I be drinking down making me come around
Special feelings whenever you're in my arms

One glass my head goes off I cannot sleep
In my dream together we fly round on tour
It becomes so real and I want some more
Falling so deep and I'm drowning in love

A fine wine filled with much for ages to last
True thick and stir we racing to top of there
Quenching form of thirst as all we provide
To last the night and for many more years

Older the sweeter I am here to collect
My fine wine, my heart select forever

CHANCE

If I trip, stumble and fall, I will rise again
I keep forging ahead to meet better days
Going through burning fire, currency low
By chance the sun will rise my way again

Climb back to days of utmost fulfilment
Cape of royalty with accessories of gold
Wine overflow as everyone takes his own
Barns filled jars at brim rejoicing overflow

Life, none knows chances tomorrow bring
Turns of events from bottom to the peak
Each man to his destiny and keys eternal
All is portrayed and known by the creator

Keep walking praying to enter better realm
Goods flowing like the sea till end of time

NIGHT

To ease off pressure many night of work
How hard can life get for survival all year
Bills yet paid in my dreams I see amount
Worse when alone leading me into trance

All night till next break of dawn in circles
Time is counting and been split into two
All that's gone parallel what's yet to come
Caught in middle the wheel keeps turning

Dark or cross to light, I choose to be bright
Like the moon shining all night giving sight
To navigate and find all that's hidden inside
Of life deeper than root of cash many crops

Keeping for now and for many more to see
Still brought to life through now and all-time

GONE

Many years gone and years to come
So are humans many more to evolve
The earth keeps spinning we revolve
Back to time of when new faces born

Walk counting work done in seconds
Tick of time never relive forward ever
Marching into line running dash of life
Wind will blow rain shower temperate

When soul transcends then it's all gone
Like bygone life is all done next in view
Oblivion with no means to relate earth
The spirit is gone to place no one know

We live for breathe the lungs can keep
And for steps the leg can take till gone

PROMISES

Take my all, down the aisle we become one
Holding hand bonding hearts two turn one
A love never to worn, happy days to come
All hours of the day a smiling face is born

No thinnest of reasons to cause a frown
Happiness fills the day I'll be your clown
Causing laughter's bringing so much joy
Cuddling through the night out on foyer

I promise to be your sun, star and moon
Making light in dark of days and swoon
Closest to your heart and be your Woon
Dancing to beautiful rhythm of life tune

Going into years from now until forever
Same promises to be kept now till ever

LOST IN DUST

Sight grave I behold and can never forget
A view of life in critical becoming so thin
Tiny particle like atom boom, spring forth
It's all bone, the greatest of all turns dust

In peak of silence the world speaks mute
No more pain as receptors changes code
Trumpets will sound or is it a silent flute
All mortals eating, one day growing old

Dust to dust and man will be lost in dust
Years of toiling, digging to place of rest
Into deep of earth, a place of no speech
New life is to begin, with so much still

Time go counting forward it never end
Gone to never return like dust in wind

FALL IN

Many more walk and miles yet to cover
Many fly out of radar, work undercover
Creating shades to distort bright rays
Hide in shadows monochrome colors

Climbing mountains, hiking self-made
Search for all that's hidden, man-made
Striking hard rock for wisdom to spring
Gushing out revealing words till eternity

And one day good things all fall in place
To replace years of struggles and dark
Showing steps to take as lights spark
Create prints keeping images in space

A long journey to end of one's future
Persistence, good will fall in destiny

RAINY

Little drops of water wetting floor I stand
Deep in desert, climates misunderstand
Deep in my heart I pray rains do not stop
Although slippery still I climb to the top

Little drops of water falling from blue sky
Wash away bad thoughts from my head
Clean my thinking and make my soul new
To receive healing I come in morning dew

Heavy drops of water to make grass green
Wash away evil roots and make town clean
Farmers after they sow pray for rains to fall
Crops growing tall so is the human wishes

Rainy season bringing abundant of good
Rainy season covering farms with green

SOURCE

Whence does the air we breathe come from
How does wind get energy moving to-n-fro
Nature on earth I see leading me to ponder
From where do source to sustain life come

Birds of the air fishes of species under sea
In the wild animals of carnivore, herbivore
Humans some meek, acting temperament
Some filled with ill roaming non jurisdiction

Searching for the source intellect emanate
Following the star, I gaze crossing borders
Like pigment wanting multicolor from life
I read writings on walls deep in my sleep

Going back to Supreme who created all
Source from where my thinking is borne

REWIND

Work hours of the day, man needs rewind
A walk to seaside and seeing ocean tides
Heavy waves as big ships go passing by
A soothing relief to my once busy mind

Profits to be made then it go down drain
I and my spirit fight, feeling deep of pain
At night I find a spot, ease muscle pulls
Blow of tensions and fragments of hate

Rewind to a point the journey go smooth
Hurdles they disappear as I think good
The sun will arise bringing me nutrients
Shining bright and I become energized

When life throws unknown shades at me
I go for rewind to relax myself from heat

MORNING

Night time is dark but morning will come
Pocket may be dry but money will come
Keep working like gardener always tends
And watch the morning come so bright

Day turns dark for one to sleep and rest
Close eyes and begin dreaming of best
Don't stutter great men underwent same
Because morning time will surface again

Mourning time wouldn't last a whole year
Even crying eye will someday become dry
Bland? One day it'll turn becoming tasteful
Blank? One day my words will be on marble

Staying awake at night contrasting ways
Knowing in few hours morning will arise

WHEEL

SACRED

Connecting to a source that never run dry
From where it all comes, closer I go and try
Reach high to God and the sun will shine
Knowing way through life I come out fine

Words to be written vision seen, it's clear
Face my fear to researching more I dare
Centuries more to come filled with ideas
As to when life will change wheels' steer

Sacred and written down deep in words
Seeing handwritings divine on the board
A dash from birth until my trumpet calls
Guides I will need why I look up to God

Life race eternal, final creation to come
Keeping commandments till sundown

STORM

On smooth sail abruptly comes stormy sea
Waves high as mountain splash and I see
To put things right the past is left behind
Hurt from sting and to calm thoughts hot

On smooth sail the wind blows once again
To new destination paddling through tides
Deep of the night moonlight giving sight
Calming fight between man and inner self

Storms will arise, balanced I keep pushing
Up blue sky down blue waters life is blue
Bringing anew feelings to forge in metal
Strong withstanding toughest of storms

Time keeps tick like ocean flowing nonstop
Through ups and down heading to the top

STEADFAST

Morning, the sun arises bringing new hope
Daunting, a place things do not seem right
Flaunting, government make citizen's envy
Hauling away good they bring dark waves

Cost of living rising up for those in average
Leaders in abundance and neglect to care
Can life ever get sweet like cola beverage?
Pushing through all without shakes 'n' fear

Steadfast I remain to life path and destiny
Going atop hills to know distance I'll cover
Working years to years till life turns bright
Black turn blue shining light up in the sky

Resolute loyalty to earnings now till ever
Divine energy I keep going till happiness

NEXT DOOR

One door closes a thousand doors open
To opportunity coming with more token
Risk taken and man was made of pure
Breaking ether rain showers and it pour

Next door locked, hold patience it open
Into a new realm from where it's Cullen
Calling, voice keeps directing to renew
Spirit, body and one soul all turn anew

Next door to new path all I see is best
Steps taken to surviving time and test
Turn of climate, deep in desert it rain
Abundance, it flows quenching thirst

Past locked future written yet to come
Till decay going through one final door

YEARS

From a distance standing to see instance
How time rotates and bringing memories
Flashing through with much of credence
Honing many thoughts and new theories

Feverish, the wind blows changing course
Healing to come, refreshing of new pulse
Faint of heart but strength will charge up
Heat through night breeze calms the tide

Feelings lasting to million years coming
Hindrance will but try reaching no avail
For time alone tells with a ticking heart
Happy moment to last hung with frame

For you alone I stick turning to stone
However it may come going to years

DEFEAT

Fire, brimstone, cold ice falling to earth
Man work hard every day fighting death
Economy so unclean causing more dirt
A time for well spending causing upset

Rage in many forming turning to vices
To create ways of survival and devices
Destabilize norms, shrinking of biceps
Energies channeling on wrong railway

Defeat faced, the feet takes new stand
Positive to lead everyone in this band
One-day singing songs of glory sound
Rejoicing through on new road bound

Ringed with defeat I punch and bend
Time bringing results on earth spent

BROKEN

Lonely, my eyes are broken I see the star
When down I come up like shining star
Thoughts go wider 'n' now I'm seeing far
Soar higher up swimming in brighter sky

Accidents occur and falling down to earth
Deep in sleep and all I wish for, new rebirth
New breath bouncing forward out in turbo
Speed of life as wheel of time spin onward

Broken to heal the mind spirit body and soul
One large field and one day the bucket kick
Fore then man work round to achieve goals
Growing old lots of fun walk holding stick

Whole in tunes of life and melody it brings
Broken records fixed and the music play

WRITINGS

Sudden writings on the wall showing way
Directions yet to come showing laid trail
Close concave to see clear like telescope
Stunning events calligraph save for future

For he that pay attention to receive signal
Fission of thoughts pull through so lethal
What's to come bigger than all-time gone
History saved in imaginations can't burn

Writings on the wall closed eyes see clear
Midst of dark alphabets bright form light
Three thousand years come it still shines
Send deep meanings into future of earth

Keep right illuminate inner god light
Positive mind nature smiling all night

SPACE

Each microsecond passing life turns on
Crossing milestone time keep burns on
Matter of things all fall down in gravity
Balcony seated sipping thru in brevity

Revving brain with jet power lit up high
Into sky, search for all yet to be found
Twenty-four hour and the years' count
Find comfort in space, journey bound

Blue clouds many words live in space
Change of weather days cloudy it rain
Heat felt in different lives unique face
Some broken find words to heal pain

Footprints of lives kept up in space
Wheels turning event they resurface

TUNNEL

Tunneling through challenges thus far
To find glory end of day roads camber
Curves from turns working for balance
Boring to find solutions calm of anger

Cutting deep into earth organic grow
Knowledge from seed sown all guide
A hole leading one into great success
Final divinity crowned king of essence

Tunneling connecting wrongs to right
Experience returns back karma soothing
Clock ticking like sounds of life rhythm
Portal created, all to find good thinking

Tunneling thru history past to present
Traces of data predicting what's next

ROLLING

Time, like a wheel rolling on earth surface
Journey of circles, some face rough days
Midst of struggle strive on to new ways
Breathe from afresh one new revolution

Turn power from oppression time is here
Rotating factor for young to come near
Era of digital mind set, what they fear
Gone are times of dark from blind set

Dice of life cast energy take me up six
Reach time of peak eating lovely steaks
Living free in a place filled garden green
Sweet peace elements tuned in harmony

Coming from past brushing forward path
New life rolling riding on marked up roads

DAWN

Each passing day man wakes to new sun
Highway humans walking going to places
In bright all toil till night for pleasant rest
The moon take turn revealing more grace

Vision scream, more work yet to be done
Large dream showing future yet to come
Rose to meet, on vacation travel and tour
Far finding sweet love that never go sour

Break of dawn to new living from reform
Healing pure motivates to do some more
Being a bread winner, till day of final call
Standing tall offspring takes new height

Dawn, ushering man into another realm
Ticking time stops spirit go to no return

FUN

In summer sun hanging out having fun
Giving all I want things money can't buy
Walked far-n-hard now we come this far
Feelings to stay a love given back repay

Gone to sun so hot and it begins to burn
Blazing fire multiple turn skin don't burn
Bond strong million miles keep going on
Smiles all over heart days filled with fun

Riding on oceans your eyes like blue sea
Passion bursting forth flows no restricts
Giggles hickles goosebumps more fore
Skin tanning lounging cooling body heat

Growing old never cold engine blow hot
On fun rides uncaged emotions set free

JUNGLE

Going past tall trees shrubs jumping monkey
Running faster aiming for brighter 'n' money
Wallow long searching for way out of jungle
Making bundle of currency note they dangle

Rustle rattles wanting to spit danger venom
Looking to sky knowing one day I Phenom
Bustle forestry deep night stargaze new life
Clearing path working to pay ultimate price

Living non-living all cluster to block track
Divert out to innovative for one eyes only
Google to map large hectares remaining
Solid mining deep mind make a way out

Traces of flags signs turning left or right
Jungle of life year's count up to success

ENERGY

I'll rise; long journey life decides to take
Day after day going still place new stake
Energy as fuel to propel mechanic engine
Around like degrees going in three sixties

Count step, mountain high reaching top
Food as energy less body dissect to part
Tearing apart a whole source from one
Nothing is destroyed, energy never loss

Bloodline spirits of forefathers in DNA
Energy from root up in sky of branches
Fountain of spring offshoot larger clan
Deep in ground, organic where life live

A view of whence man is made appear
Create divine from omnisource no fear

MOMENT

Flash of transconcious riding high wave
Rising tide problems they all run by dry
Sun shining brighter, day's tears of brave
Fall in rain wash pain more gain to buy

Time running fast ten years like a day
Picture keeping memories words I say
In art recreate juicing out more green
In books time past present keep keen

Different values of life, deep it means
Moments all retain pass to next of kin
And baton is release a new race begin
Smile so diverse happiness on all face

Cherish with so much love and value
Moments stored in deepest of heart

TURN POINT

Future search balance to tilt on either end
Electron repel turn to direction road bend
Working to repair of every share being fair
Take step build castle and protected heir

Toiling earth look to sun till turning point
Wheel of years flower beautiful grow fine
Save up in trickles holding massive coin
Cover huge land mass kilometers long

Bright Light shine dark is seen no more
Multi-color of emotions covered in fur
Body mind spirit soul summing to fore
Heal all sore rivers and fountain pour

Turn to new standing point sea view
Like waters flow so is words to man

LIFE

Life experience to learn I take down note
In phase working daily from part to whole
It rotates round in circle your turn my turn
Neither scared of up nor down face front

Days draw by tears germinate glory seed
All sorrow gone like joy of new baby born
Harvest to come season fall into position
Many rejoicing for alas big family is form

Peace of heart portraying beautiful souls
Replicas blood continuum black like coal
Words sacred voice listen jump into flow
Better times arrive calendar count grow

Seated at a position life of view so clear
Projectile flight, make use of energy here

ERA

Life giving a break time goes to relapse
Do not give in new day sun will rise again
Shining light everyone bright huge strides
New info knowledge yet found we search

Up in cloud new language of era we find
Man talking to machine millions connect
Real-time server to store into many years
Keep memories of programs man-made

What time to be alive in technology age
Fortune to be made early techies smile
Digital mind syntax and logic to follow
Code written down thru window it flow

Era of time things unthinkable is done
Like in Silicon Valley many Ideas born

RESTART

Time stand still events pause wind blow
Away from enemy many disguise, all foes
Make more though keeping things fallow
Keep all surroundings clean with a hoe

Barns to fill responsibility needed to fill
Mountains and hill, raising leg and kneel
Prayers for soul to heal bitter turn sweet
Challenges come in midst breaking free

To restart different turns from life to pick
To mend cut down trees and broken stick
Retrieve blur roads going to shady corner
Nor accident bend, linear, straight, proper

Each tick back to zero there life restart
In second past of time where it's found

MANDIAS

RUNNING

Running away from dark pulling me back
Pick up great pieces and make high stack
Past worries dead in dreams they go grave
Running breaking boundaries to top brave

Climbing mountain cold weather touch sky
Wider horizons high clouds images say hi
Walking far no slow pace steps double up
Journey of time seconds tick running up

Chase after end of destiny filled with smile
Larger family to dine with, worth the while
Beauty of handworks summing to assets
Future go unending circle keep its turning

Like cart pulled by a horse time is running
Into new faces to come when we all gone

MANDIAS

Take center stage standing tall like martyr
To protect all watch road like Ozymandias
Like statue, come rain come sun it remain
Inanimate seeing as things begin uproar

Counting keeping record wind turns vane
Directions it points spirits go making hay
Yet unshaken concrete foot never move
Head up high and seen by a button click

View how far as to where the journey leads
Years in open field now covered by dream
From the past to good and beautiful scene
Till filling enlarged capacity to keep feeling

I am Mandias tourist far near come to see
Photos and to save memories never forget

APOCALYPSE

Whirl wind spinning globe and earth rotate
Eclipse of the sun to last a thousand days
Mountains dating back age keep growing
Voices in harmony all clamor to be free

Dread sights never to behold in lifetime
Tears mixed form colors and w'all paint
Wash to monochrome, spectrum views
Clanging metals warriors best and new

Fight through apocalypse time sun rise
Melting ice breaking chains bound cold
Taking steps, work to draw image bold
Life across, Eden like sheep and flock

Night but lasting dusk-dawn we strive
Struggle time vanish in coming hours

REVERENCE

Culture religion ways of human existence
Five days a week it ends with persistence
Detail of time each day working to spend
Reverence to Creator all-knowing till end

On the road to become obstacles to jump
Race to run for many years' blood'll pump
From roots with stump fruits they'll grow
Water to sow rainfall, rivers high and flow

For let it be so as dreams turning reality
Rocky road and in cold moment's frailty
Reverence to trials and all up in the past
As change's constant for nothing to last

Reverence on road and beauty of nature
Featured in life cast its reasons to unfold

MOULD

Run and flight jump and soar more to come
Things to be done, many trends to perform
Moulding step, mountain high splitting cleft
Burnt as with brick hard prints for a rebirth

Into years of sunshine thoughts be strong
Carve history and for trace in words long
Circle spin future takes mould into form
Hardened to formation visual art is born

Experience, emotion ingredients like clay
Blast sands of time keep record in space
Blue, rainbow colors and all blend in poet
Refreshing value lasting years like Moët

Moulding path for next to see, reference
Paving way to life journey recorded in art

GIANT STEP

Making move breaking through hard knock
Life brick built high up to cover future sight
Intentional staying on track go beyond luck
Big foot marching on to time winning fight

Unique shoe size and task to trample upon
Solutions to find searching far from home
Journey into space and earnings to live-on
Acts to keep arts to relive found in chrome

Giant step prints on earths' surface to last
Flows in bloodstream its ink never run dry
Next generations follow suite running fast
Pass mark and new world of happy dream

Stamp from past guide direction to come
Good better best, chronology of all times

KING

Made divine seated atop throne of words
Creating art bringing live what's not seen
Beauty to behold keenly events do unfold
Gate opens everyone into success they go

Paved roads humans into good life drive
Land green all what you lay hand survive
Living the dream journey a thousand mile
Working to keep document and asset file

Kingdom to come you and I be the King
Mass choir sweet melodies we all sing
Stories written on the palm of our hand
On sands of time printed to see the end

Registered with a smile for years to last
Path onto phase era of time King is born

FORTUNE

Travel far and wide into jungle being's wild
To find future of time when all thing bright
Across landmines and dangers all around
Faced with a smile research to see if real

Dark sky yet not relent going to better day
Till ground wanting to reach water spring
Through heat of past thoughts to be calm
Accelerate to destination of ones' destiny

Arrive a point it all makes deepest sense
Gushing of currencies world make sense
Philanthropy beyond immediate of family
Controlling direction and to where spend

God-given fortune value never depreciate
Years onto years like gold it goes up high

CIRCUS

Circus show large wheel turning, this life
Connected pipes to all oxygen for deliver
Pump to motion character and deceiver
Events come many more to go take five

Round to make security to check safety
Drift from damage problem less weighty
Smiles for keep to cheers and all hearty
Dance into new show strong and mighty

Lights turn-off curtain fall end of circus
Experiences, memories lots more done
Blink of eye set no more vanity all gone
Image long remain, body soul oblivious

Hullabaloo Journey to beyond for tour
All kept behind to make life circus fun

PROTECTOR

Dark lights pandemonium new being is born
Midst of war or wants boy keeps growing fast
Warriors' slain, thundering downpour of rain
Gnashing and tears, family migrate for more

Path to freedom challenge circle to obstruct
Push through the wall aim sanity and vision
Mission to lead sailing sea, spirit direct vane
Journeying to thought island lesson to gain

New form and existence lot means to survive
To end of procrastination life sweet as honey
Force coming to positive aligns all things right
Paving way to time offspring's' best of buddy

Protector of name hold blood print of past
Character and new traits generation to last

DISTURBIA

Crying wolves flying doves run round circles
Unveil to reveal million paths make one cycle
Locked up in cage roar waiting for time it tell
View from high colors dim not many a- smile

Disturbed mind sleepless night movie replay
Broken sticks lit up woods life burns in array
Hunger and cries government acts of chary
One-day life turn, glimpse upon new parley

Turbo on new lane out of past new horizon
Flying soon to moon make strong all weary
Better is tomorrow for making of art to last
Fast, all heart prosper to distance non-solo

Disturbia sounds and creeping movement
No avail light is come, time shine so bright

SMILE

Years to race on earth to live world to build
Empty man is born experiences to be filled
Sometime mislead retracing back to start
Keeps hope alive pushing till heartbeat flat

Strike and venom broken ground loophole
Misdemeanor putting futures on high pole
Stakes fly up, amounts waiting lucky day
Hard work put in earnings and way of pay

Smile going through current waiting next
Earth to refine clock drills into world best
Beauty in time is kept marching into glory
Memories kept in tales and written story

Smile to brighten the night sending spark
Smile to gladden the mind make it bright

LOYALTY

Might go offside loyalty put me on track
Ball in court reasoning holding me back
Decisions to form and brave steps make
Life as oven and be cooking best of cake

Bonding to future speed dial and rocket
Loyalty boosts up end, meeting far near
Compass giving direction in gold locket
Distances to memories brought so dear

Keeping in mind that good feeds loyalty
Images of better to spur multiple actions
Clothing of garments made from royalty
Turning outcome to best a new mission

Takes two to form ingredient for loyalty
Like salt and pepper so is me and you

BOUND

Bound on this journey called life days' end
Meander through experience it never stop
Sunrise till sundown- many come and go
Tales to be told words written on marble

Faced with shapes and multi-color of life
Retrace steps to new lane success bound
Balance on edge look far reaching sound
Echo of pasts to disrupt one smooth jive

Like rocket flight bound into sky seamless
Lay hands on creativity turning dream full
Craft a world imaginable strike eye of bull
Bring to reality words love and sweetness

Road to afterlife tip take and turn to make
Into happy days we all cheer growing old

GOOD

Life gets good, digging and find sweetness
Like born in spring new flowers they grow
Taste on buds' reality occur power to flow
Going in time through haze and blindness

Steps to take, striking rock fountain shoot
So is good in depth of a man lock in heart
Path to strive happiness to find everlasting
Shadows ignite for all man happy rejoicing

Abundant of good falling from sky to earth
Refresh the mind varieties travel the world
Currency to spend memory all things good
Joy to remain on imprints fashion and art

Frontiering imaginations future we see
Lot of good kept till planted seeds grow

DEEP

Dip in potion covered waiting to reveal
Stir to fry free thinking all deep 'n' roast
Moves and toast brotherhood and chill
Clear of coast and shore landing is sure

Deep sea mining, find gold in rough day
Deeper you go and clearer life become
Split second of thought never to come
A beacon eyes caught pain felt no more

Inking blood mix passion burn as fuel
Dead cell and twitching burn like hell
Image come future is bright and clear
Rays and spectrum declare com earth

Deep it never stops embedded in art
From deep it come on a road I know

SAVOUR

Faced it all savour glory to end of days
Battles never to fall, working till it pays
Chanting for victory sweet like grapes
Coming from ancient with knows old

Clinking glasses toast to modern way
Integrated, man display future ability
Technique to resolve lost in labyrinth
Savour found path until the end of air

Refreshing it remains until evergreen
Generation sees, standing tall always
Unbeaten words truthful all guiding
Drinking down quench insatiability

Savour peace and happiness coming
To stay forever till sun stops shining

LIGHT

I am light like sunshine each breath I take
Sending beams illuminate mind and rake
Scratch surface dig deep to find resource
Look up to God created as god one force

Never to hide reaching wide and all place
Emotions to read passion written on face
Many years and the star keep shine light
Dim and to arise sun coming shine bright

You are light emancipate sight boundary
Blue sky million live in steel like foundry
Everlasting words shining light touch life
Memories form generation come afterlife

Continuum of human characters alive
Come to noon in the dark shine light

TALL

Long years gone, tree by seaside flourish
Far to time photosynthesis and it nourish
Deep roots into culture and history come
Tapping words from stream in multi-turn

Standing tall sight above ground to cloud
Shoulder tall walking swift value of pound
Drift to position and making move visible
Art of Impressionism made to ostensible

Tall is creator with a foresight out of box
Stopping bombs and restrain evil to lock
Make good abundant materials all place
Economy go up, happiness leaving trace

The world going on new imaginations
Drawn reality knowledge stack up tall

LONELY

Lonely statue in dark stand and keep watch
Sun will rise all view speak language Dutch
Lonely road driving through search for love
One eye view god sight fore-coming no flaw

Mind to reveal a lonely world mortal is all
Journey turn planted seed grow stand tall
Shrubs to forest many come and souls go
Recorded into memories story to be told

Journey to oblivion lonely in a labyrinth
No time micro steps float through space
No faces, linear spirits go into purgatory
Time is done sound of call wipe all clean

Mandias to see back in earth he brings
Lonely he stands for years' statue reveal

PEACE & LIGHT

CROW AT DAWN

Ushering a day never seen before
Arising new opportunities present
Working to make each hour asset
Running race in 24 miles per day

Time alone tells when scars heal
Nature to blend climate's change
Pains on the road and body tells
Mission on the go reaching ends

Cock crow at dawn alarm wake up
More is to come living winning tall
In paradise overlooking a city lit up
Staying afloat challenges like traffic

Crow at dawn years counting pass
Memories of the morning to relive

NEW LIFE

Nine months of forming, wander in a womb
New life is coming ancestors meet in a tomb
Donate blood from history and to for bearer
Speak new offspring giving light to all hearer

Decision for history marathon a new runner
Energy never lost DNA to store blood owner
Trace to find source, hills mountains valley
New face born to reflect the future coming

Keeping code to find different turns, ways
New view of life seeing clear no fuzzy hays
Taking steps motion in play to better days
Family tree growing large all making pays

New fruit given, vineyard everyday toiling
Growing to return million more in profits

JOURNEY MAN

On this journey in search of illumination
To find phronesis experience come n go
Sometimes be introvert research in heart
Road tour the mind speed, go to distance

On this journey is a lot of human being
Of made characters and destiny it lights
Same path I find one to love with desire
Reaching turn hold hands across bridge

Journey to end of time beauty in dream
Working to make worthwhile, best team
Little a droplets come together and big
Step taken not in vain seed grow like fig

Euphoria, reminisce of moments lived
Journey of images kept buried in sand

CASTLE

King return banquet filled with rejoicing
Soldiers dancing warriors for rewarding
Wine overflow taste of victory is certain
Cheers to spoils of campaign, war tour

Night till daylight celebration ceaseless
Enemy fallen time of spring and sunrise
Look out window beautiful face endless
Habitation back normal thing of no price

Seat at mountain top glow unto heaven
Bright and bold perfect like rays of light
Guide through the night for no sleeping
Stand front protecting wall for all living

All night at castle top, wind of thoughts
Divine protection for man is but mortal

STAIN

Made from dust blood passion form blend
New bond done reflections to see far end
Like mirror showing a life none omit stain
Mission through hurdles one can see pain

Decision wrong mistake appear on white
Deter from pattern how to cure one blight
New dot occur time to take road of repent
Go away from who deceives like a serpent

A stain that leads to derailment from pure
Stain on culture from foreign made to cure
Re-clean wash thought devices and habit
Able to see coming directions and gambit

Rescue bring back roots of development
Wash stains on human, mind be set free

LOST WORLD

From fire ice spring forth turn cold then heat
Allegory seeing in faint thirsty need more fill
View in opaque paddle across deep blue sea
To find gold, riches of man travel to hills top

Circle of wind strong digging deep into earth
Whirl hole portal open visualize outer realm
Floating souls market square trading of lives
Old to new face, bygones for many are stale

Lost world hidden away from ordinary eyes
Price and exchange each one a soul it count
Puzzle and riddle to solve finding a way out
Retrace not found dimensions on new path

Dust tell source of energy direction bound
Find way to earth revisiting once a life end

GRAIL

Dress in gold diamond coated precious stone
Value until bone like fountain deep unending
Knowledge for keep awake at night searching
Hand to receive Holy Grail message take home

The wisest is not he who stays away all alone
Surrounded multi-facet watch like eagle eye
Not to fall prey, keeping life line of currency
Wisdom to relate in words kept makes a way

Innovate for there is unique in every being
Out of the box read fly high see write down
Vision reveal road paved challenge appear
Skid through the rain bold and face all fear

Grail, inspired, open receives all to come
Portion to drink let my cup run overflow

DIAMOND

Normand thinking hidden so deep in heart
To core of earth hot many a struggles spat
Priceless, child eyes of tears giving a smile
Frame up high reveal time of war n search

Blood thirst landing for diamonds buried
Charge upon hills exhume, no stones left
Following a map incorrect a mind of theft
Camp confused soldiers all sit so worried

Sanctimony diamond leader takes throne
Protecting heritage bring peace and light
Words to motivate defeat opposing sides
Secure future for the young with fortunes

Cries wiped away all hail sun giving bright
Like diamond have heart crystalline pure

PLANET EARTH

Circle of life it goes around God planned
Man created to disrupt with gun n bomb
Living ruins climate clouded in pollution
Corrupt practices unfair trade in market

Downplayed value for peaceful existence
Many remain positive fill with persistence
Spill from toxic, ocean with plastic covers
Epoxy binding man in need, new lifestyle

Fair use of planet for generation to come
Rivers running dry water source in threat
Efficiency decline for earth need a rebirth
From dictators and warlords blood rulers

Take me back to green love of vegetation
A round table to make earth whole again

WIDE

Abyss to reconcile, humans drifting apart
Lens for capture into forests wide of wild
Life all is part come together make whole
Days to nightfall many voices clearer call

Bond form as clay, dust from wide come
Positive to charge emitting rays in turns
Wider thoughts is gone climb seeds tall
Germinate some more ideas all in word

Treading across rift communicate uplift
Horizons wide over fence look and see
Out of labyrinth resolute in conscience
Open blood cell red flow making mortal

Wide range of emotions perception view
Link to connect like last piece in a puzzle

REPURPOSE

Crying wolves flying doves run round circles
Unveil to reveal million paths make one cycle
Locked up in cage roar waiting for time it tell
View from high colors dim not many a- smile

Disturbed mind sleepless night movie replay
Broken sticks lit up woods life burns in array
Hunger and cries government acts of chary
One-day life turn, glimpse upon new parley

Turbo on new lane out of past new horizon
Flying soon to moon make strong all weary
Better is tomorrow for making of art to last
Fast, all heart prosper to distance non-solo

Disturbia sounds and creeping movement
No avail light is come, time shine so bright

SONNET OF A TRAVELER

Through the forest run angry wolves attack
Jumping log falls and rolls hard break back
Ghost of past chase want grab for entwine
Cast thee away sending evil back to swine

Dark night rowing boat Sea begins uproar
Waves high and low, sharks sea lions roar
Boat capsize middle of ocean a dead see
Sinking to bottom for trip transcends fee

Ride on cloud angel wings, everyone bow
Carpet on ground royalty found to endow
Reality obscure eyes treated looking afar
Years ahead for events to play hole a par

Traveler alien and back, in storms stand
Motion bound and not to cease till end

VENUS

Form divine with beauty of a god
Eyes full of love strike open a pod
Seed sown deep in heart, your arm
I want to lie in, protect from harm

Striking a pose no one can resist
Strong armies at look face defeat
A call upon Venus to restore love
Down high echelon rays all above

Goddess, love arrow pierce heart
Bleed out passion, emotion last
Pleasure, ground's set die is cast
Healing run through sensual pet

Riverside, goddess Venus appear
Cupid singing songs ends all fear

PRECIOUS

Mining deep down to find true emotion
Tilt at edge, fall to sea drown in potion
A sinking ship, for love to keep afloat
Older we better, hold hands row boat

Never to depart stick across centuries
Blood and form precious like cowries
Bond grow stronger forever like gold
Your warmth I cherish, a mortal bold

Precious is moment of song and cold
Years unfold our escapades be retold
Purest ever found she walk this earth
Smiles, joy all year round giving birth

More life to come standing firm in you
A love so refreshing like morning dew

PEACE DIVINE

Many lives have come, restless and they go
Strait of troubles, evil horns and they blow
Trumpet sounds, arise and find your light
Shining path unto days until turn to night

Tongues who spite like razor they cut life
Walk in darkness a mind buried in ground
Wishing to cut great destiny, seed to grow
Inflicting pains like demons they possess

Midst of all I find my peace from divine
A calm soul working to create, innovate
Experiences replay mistake not to make
Living till old a large family cutting cake

Mind on earth and all manmade to feel
None to be judged, fluid flowing like sea

RITE OF PASSAGE

Rite of passage, go to great beyond
Effervescent of dust mixed returns
Disintegrate thoughts and to bond
Body, spirit and soul pure like Nun

Historical ways be evidence of time
Like seeds in line growing to be fine
Bright of light and passage appears
Whirling portal open to protect fear

Creep in, grind digging to find ways
Blood and signs to currency for pay
Sweat all night, for humans devoid
Essence, fragrance, colors Polaroid

Up away gone leaving behind track
Passage to find in knowledge kept

SAILING

From the creeks, sailing unto Atlantic
Nocturnal moon give light and pacific
Rowing, warriors beat drums of chant
A fight for freedom, sail move like ant

War canoe we land on Akassa ground
Break through deception years bound
'To die by sword better than of hunger'
Wealth taken, and keep poor -monger

Decisive we stand ending oppression
On our waters we sail to regain rights
Reclaim inheritance, all of possession
Sing burning hoja spirits to cure blight

Battle water cannons fire, we keep sail
Last of blood we spill for ours unborn

ROCKING BOAT

Rocking boat dancing to rhythm of wave
Sound of engine like drum beat concave
Calling, birds echo and regatta come out
Like summer at riverside paddle and row

Rocking boat, ups and down such is life
Stand strong deep foot in seas like jetty
No more cry happiness wipe away petty
Clash, clang, clans spread wide across

Rocking boat till old live in love till cold
Holding hand history be told of growth
Seeds sown into future, light is thrown
From high god is known gold is shown

Rock-a-bye going to oblivion work done
Next born to relive protect what is come

ETERNAL

Eternity reveals on same path walking
Nature stalking keep record of talking
Hear whispers trespass new boundary
Blood form like iron from new foundry

To eternal chase of good and what all
Leap and strides on pyramid stand tall
Knowledge, seek light at end of tunnel
Streamline life like oil through a funnel

Engines rotate air to fuel till lights out
Cup overflow into a new realm of time
Close eye and see millennium in sand
Image germinate to eternal it resound

Seconds past never to return, it's done
Eternal, destination for all mortal born

OTHER SIDE

Peaceful night reflect of images on sky
Read through hidden lines of high facts
Mysteries and spice on other side of life
Glimpse, pipe chimney burning incense

Lullaby angelic voices and they all sing
Soothing sound relax the mind no think
Cross finish line, a heart pacing it relax
Savor time of victory from bill and pay

Faces smile from ground, peaceful arise
Other side of life all white beauty appear
No stains from spill, emotion kept intact
Floating dead and alive in market to buy

Buried in ground side of world unknown
Seeds they sprout sign of good we know

MYST

WITHEREST

Bloom of the morning flowers like rose
Fly up in the sky as sun, soar with dove
Out on the plains, active about all goes
Vane show direction to ancestral home

Across hilly riding, reach mountain toe
In Witherest we all work till growing old
Family to care for, market to win bread
Digging with a hoe, persevere find gold

Buried deep in Witherest state of mind
Cognitive, ascertain clay for moulding
Drilling to spring unending happy days
Celebrating years of hard work returns

Drawing source to earth blood as ink
Painting Witherest a world to reveal

14 SAINTS

Peace be to you lover of Mother Nature
Peace be to thee whose words are loved
Peace unto you, martyr sacrificing a life
Strength to you who go about for peace

Health to thee who search for knowledge
Health to thee who find and write process
Wealth to thee who create with thy hands
Wealth to thee who trade in just principle

Scent of victory as the years flowing past
Bend of history, saints gather in mystery
Revealing destiny and path we all follow
Rising to glory as stones cast hang in air

Homing, time on earth ticking calling spirit
14 saints in cloak turning unto generations

MYSTICAL

Creation of existence endowed in oxygen
Clay as particles wind blows into process
Man is made to form complex psychology
Emotions toss yet it returns a blood gene

Made as star walking on surface of earth
Like electricity power up a shining mind
Brightly sight working onto heavenly path
On destination ride to vanity, end of pride

Mystically a world operating on said rule
Palm rub palm making something huge
Friction to challenge, man's sailing thru
Cross and star farmer tilling the ground

To mystic order, place we are all bound
Historically man is made and oblivious

VALLEY

Scorching sun, drought, valley of dry bones
Clanging metals defending arm annexation
Blood sucking ruler insatiable, more lands!
Suppressing free lives, refugee on increase

Valley of mixing light, exorcisms heal patch
Down into tunnel of reset call for a rematch
New count, soldiers wake with revived mind
Battle at bottom now rising up in helium air

Illuminate, monastery of knowledge appear
Entrant at valley, climbing to mountain top
Mastery, every soul loud gaining one voice
Winning battles at valley, en-route to God

A world of peace, ending act like Rus-here
Signing love pact, free is one, free is for all

MONTEGO

Pour more till all cup is filled to the brim
Strategy yielding result like tailored trim
Chocolate, vanilla cream, all in machine
Sweetness from within, grapes and pie

Let's merry for tomorrow we sail on sea
Into deep, heavens and the ocean meet
Suckling to feed, home keeper's behind
Goodbye Montego for never'e shall see

Next day to strive we were born for life
To inherit all fight and celebrating alive
Mind on price, through swamp not shy
Impure linen washed with tears of joy

Goodbye Montego a wonder of the sea
Deep in rosy bed no air still we breathe

BLUE STAR

Aye! Captain look, b.l.u.e s.t.a.r in blue sky
Do we speed up the engine and then fly?
Words are floating showing nautical path
The horizon is lit up broad and now bright

Look! Over there dolphins out they dance
Wave is calm, a coincidence of the night
Omen is right the portal will open wide Sir
Running out of time Blue sky turn to sand

Rev the engine rocket and float with cloud
Going past nine, we dinner at clock of ten
There! Are alphabets, follow b.l.u.e s.t.a.r
It shall lead to place of enlightened mind

Letters to capture and phrase making life
Right Sir! Engine fired mission looks good

REACHER

Survived gallows, revolutions, twist of time
In frame of life decades past, future prime
Currency to find rock to break mould brick
Once to be slain, di-vine air becomes thick

Accuser turn sick confusions in their midst
Do not harm thee who sow peaceful seeds
Farming knowledge to cover earthly green
Into centuries seen, ideas like forest field

Reaching into mist assemble fragments
All good that's to keep for p-artly purpose
Performing, renewable energy from God
Knowing man on earth as memory store

Millenniums come, still mining for more
Reacher born deep in poetry he is form

CONNECTED

Hanging on the ledge lifeline to be heard
Tran sailing, paddle to meet a life ahead
All deeds and words said reviving dead
Ash turn green leaves float in the wind

Plugged into socket, connect to stream
Energies and they wave vibrating to red
Images resurface, mathematic to solve
Solution informs, open parting the sea

Across strait to a place wisdom installs
Now living straight and soaked in grace
Driving safe navigating highways of life
Connected from past, secure to eternal

Bouncing one more time, determination
Absorbing shock in a connected system

CONSISTENT

Staying glued to a fact that oxygen is life
Shoes stacked in rack, a journey of past
Puzzle and attack defending of the night
Creeps in crevice from within old craters

Seed is buried, in consistent soil it grow
Nor for the leaf to perish, dry and it blow
In soul is kept thought from head to sole
Jump through hurdle escaping manhole

It all repeat, consistent is determination
Key to unlocking a world of possibilities
Optimism as bread to feed, drinking wine
Night falls, at sunrise we'll go once again

In search for treasures and hidden lines
For one day we shall find heart desires

SARAFINA

Wholesomely made put in African skin
Lasting for centuries, non-expiration tin
Emotion created and to be deeply filled
Lock of dread my memory instantly feel

Sarafina, I wish to remain in your blood
Through the red and white ups n down
Beauty to declare pigment for next gen
Oh! In your eyes a new world is formed

Many come n some go but non is sticky
Tricky, wanting to capture God true love
Made in pair you hold the pleasant part
Sarafina, one more time and I am gone

The pains of inscribing you on my skin
Like tattoo glued to inner depth of love

EMPTY STREET

Walking down alley of grave loneliness
Avenue, track to find renewed mentality
Tarred road, humans making hay in day
They're all ghosts cos we end up empty

Building left in dirt, rubbles as ant food
Crumble, what we are fed in four years
In such a place good struggles for life
Choked in the night of an empty world

Empty street, single soul on a journey
To rebuild success, beautiful structure
Emancipated, discrete and realization
For a fool's mind can't be a full mind

Facing challenges and be squared on
Finding companion to make life worth

DEEP DOWN

Deep down in a whirl hole, unending base
Survival optimum crossing different phase
Broken heart, tears turn ice running a race
Amounting to unknown and future in haze

Never to give up, and moulding along fall
Heed to intuition record God calling voice
Working to limit, the night is for mind rest
Parachute, it releases paving way to land

Breaking in new realm and falling to more
Albeit, assets to speak louder than words
For bloodline to pick up, benefit of labor
Stored in the cloud, memory and nature

Deep down, a search to find what's lost
Long as air remain, a mind turn to seed

CELESTIAL

Made from high, a light shine creating life
Object like diamond reflecting God divine
Breaking of spine, wrestle and deep fight
For Victorios, Adie Mos and Contaferous

Feline, portray back never to touchdown
Celestial, spirit filled conjuring thunders
Redirecting clouds pull moon o'er sides
Touching the sun energy to charge solar

Recycling of heart, update version come
Life's non-pause always navigate course
Asteroid and galaxy, it's milky and swam
Leninist and Marxist, seeds, all is buried

Highly Celestial being to make it out alive
Landing on earth, to continue once again

LOREM IPSUM

To show path deep fog of morning light
Keen attention to detail of minute signal
Tracing to find its container and to bind
Spot to fit, data to store man creativity

Language general communicates code
Dialects and Boolean to function spate
If man is god machine to respond yes
Else the world is left to sorrow in fate

Lorem Ipsum, come in to function here
Yield binary add color to monochrome
(){} seek and ye shall find bracket time
Make hay during day, save all memory

Life compiles many events to interpret
Process and be fine, complete is end

MYSTERY

Mystery is life, time its counting device
See today and voom! Faces see no more
Memories to savor, happiness and smile
Framed up in one's mind, epistle is told

Thousands of words can't inform set out
From where it comes, place death is form
Righteous and in all, hymn and the song
Trumpet's pump to harvest, wind; it rain

Some fall far, sudden appear close side
To remind that one day mortal takes off
Appreciating a dash from born till gone
Good times to make maximum of days

Mystery, a line across completely blank
Wave do not echo, for silence installed

SURVIVAL

Drowning deep down in ocean made by man
Stirred by corrupt minds some acting so evil
Absconds with fortune placed, survival for all
Is been taken to one and who lives faraway

Repeat gimmicks, four years new stage set
Whirling ocean to select same rotten beans
A country of theater its system going sour
Time laughing pass moving to better space

Turning spiritual we are surviving on God
And the works of thy hand, roof over head
Whole beauty of life by the maker of love
Creator of peace, the sun and the moon

Impacting place scaling through the day
Uplifting and all float to top of the chain

MAGNA

Tumultuous wind shakes the root of earth
Unbrazen and dancing to high tune of life
Ubiquitous, circle of twenty four hour day
Making count, go distant places and see

Character magna, unique species made
Skin tones and ringtone mould like clay
A drive to ether realm, cross mind seas
Arrive in myst- and firm spin to iron ore

Laid grail, unveiling space to outer way
Knight Templar burning through barrier
Water springing in trunks bearing fruits
Magna canopy to shade scorching sun

Weight in ton, still climbing pushing on
Magna world rolling, never ending one

ECHELON

Taking a ride to future years and entails
Adjust knob, clarity of vision and details
Projected slide, javelin thrown, it returns
Projectile path yet to reach echelon life

Hurdle to solve, puzzle to jump realtime
Challenges appear, means man is alive
Working to increase 'n' investing in love
Diverse's born, more number adding up

Elevator sprung, turn on button for lift
Time be going long children grown up
Like I was before now moving echelon
Liquid bulk, knowledge stalk and more

On glory throne seated up knitted world
Merry bound for many days till echelon

LOSOPHICAL

Riverside amazing blue sky over head
Water cry, splashing renewed memory
Cuddle down to receive deep healing
From ancient myth, pyramid revealing

New age reminiscing and enlightening
Rock making concrete, farming allure
Compass pointing way to knowledge
Stored in cloud encoding money pay

Philosophical trading in million ways
Spinning ball, athletic sport and arts
Entertaining game, keeping all trails
At Marina Bay surfing, water is bae

Pour more thoughts by inking word
Losophy, many more written trace

HISTORY

Two thousand years yet many more to come
Hand writing these words, blood still stored
History they come showing where I'm from
Taking me back to inform, letters as reward

In line marching on Broadway and into farm
Literary hall, ancestors' writings on the wall
From father to sons, I got some on my shelf
Word never buried, living generations come

Till the farm, grow pineapple, earth's sweet
You have what it takes, stick make stakes
Inheriting forefather, blood is always right
Fore sons to preserve, each getting better

Historical, coming from blood of writers
Twenty first century Igoni Odaga in Abua

THANKS

www.ingramcontent.com/pod-product-compliance
Lightning Source LLC
LaVergne TN
LVHW091322150826
845673LV00006B/1729

* 9 7 9 8 3 6 6 2 3 0 7 1 1 *